This
PJ BOOK
belongs to

_____

_____

PJ Library®
JEWISH BEDTIME STORIES and SONGS

To Marguerite, Annabelle, and Milan

 little bee books

A division of Bonnier Publishing
853 Broadway, New York, New York 10003
Copyright © 2016 by Barroux
First published in Great Britain by Egmont UK Limited.
This little bee books edition, 2016.
All rights reserved, including the right of
reproduction in whole or in part in any form.
LITTLE BEE BOOKS is a trademark of Bonnier Publishing Group, and
associated colophon is a trademark of Bonnier Publishing Group.
Manufactured in China LPP 0917
First Edition 10 9 8 7 6 5 4 3 2 1
Library of Congress Cataloging-in-Publication data is available upon request.
011824.2K1/B1156/A5
ISBN 978-1-4998-0444-7
littlebeebooks.com
bonnierpublishing.com

I am a polar bear.

That's me with my feet in the water near my friends.

Life is quiet and peaceful on the ice, but wait a minute—

what's that **noise?**

The ice breaks!

C K !

"We're **drifting** away!" my friends cry.

"**Hold on!**" I reply.

And then it's just the three of us,
floating in the middle of the **big blue ocean**.

We need to find a new home.
But the water goes on **forever!**

We play games to pass the time.
"I spy with my little eye,
             something beginning with W. . . . "

Wave!

The **sky darkens,**
and the **waves grow bigger.**

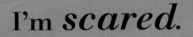

I'm *scared*.

We need to find a new home right now!

We need to find . . .

Land!
We're saved.

"Hello, cows!
We're looking for a **new home**.
May we live here, please?"

"Hmmm,
you are . . .

too **furry**."

"You are . . .

too tall."

"You are . . .

too bear-ish. Sorry!"

Off we go again,
looking for a new home.

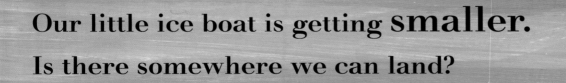

Our little ice boat is getting **smaller.**

Is there somewhere we can land?

Yes!

This could be our new home.

"Hello, panda.

May we please come ashore?"

"Hmmm, you are . . .

too **many.**

Look around, there's just not enough room!
You **can't** live here."

By the time we reach
another island, our little
ice boat has almost
melted. We don't
have much time.

"Help us!"

"Did you hear something?"

"**No.** You?"

"We could go and look."

"That's too much trouble.
Pass the **tea.**"

Things don't look good, and we're
about to give up hope when . . .

The ocean carries us to an **empty island.**
And not a moment too soon!

We have a new **home** all to ourselves.

Until . . .

"**Excuse me,**
we're looking for
a new home.

Can you help us, please?
It looks like you've got
plenty of room."

"Hmmm,
you are . . .